Library and Archives Canada Cataloguing in Publication

Cole, Kathryn, author
That uh-oh feeling : a story about touch / written by
Kathryn Cole ; illustrated by Qin Leng.

(I'm a great little kid series)
Co-published by: Boost Child & Youth Advocacy Centre.
ISBN 978-1-927583-91-3 (hardcover)

1. Touch—Juvenile fiction. 2. Secrets—Juvenile fiction.
I. Leng, Qin, illustrator II. Boost Child & Youth Advocacy Centre, sponsoring body III. Title.

PS8605.O4353T43 2016   jC813'.6   C2015-908362-1

*Boost Child & Youth Advocacy Centre gratefully acknowledges the generous support
of Rogers Communications for funding the development and publication of the Prevention
Program Series. Rogers Communications is an important partner in our efforts to prevent
abuse and violence in children's lives.*

*Second Story Press gratefully acknowledges the support of the Ontario Arts Council and the
Canada Council for the Arts for our publishing program. We acknowledge the financial support
of the Government of Canada through the Canada Book Fund.*

ONTARIO ARTS COUNCIL
CONSEIL DES ARTS DE L'ONTARIO
an Ontario government agency
un organisme du gouvernement de l'Ontario

❀ Canada Council   Conseil des Arts
for the Arts   du Canada

Funded by the Government of Canada
Financé par le gouvernement du Canada | Canadä

Published by
Second Story Press
20 Maud Street, Suite 401
Toronto, Ontario, Canada
M5V 2M5
www.secondstorypress.ca

That Uh-oh Feeling

A story about touch

written by Kathryn Cole
illustrated by Qin Leng

Second Story Press

Claire stamped her foot. "I'll *never* get this right!"

"You will," said Coach Ian. "Remember! New skills take practice."

Claire tried again. She ran forward and kicked, but the soccer ball went sideways, not toward the goal.

"Almost," Ian encouraged. "Keep at it," he called, as he hurried to set up some pylons for the kids to dribble around.

Claire frowned. *Almost isn't good enough*, she thought. Shaun and Nadia were on her team. Maybe one of them could show her what was going wrong.

"Can you help me?" she asked Shaun.

"Sure," he said, and he tried. But he really wasn't much better than Claire.

When Ian was finished setting up the pylons, he came back. "How's it going?" he asked.

"Not good." Claire frowned even more.

Ian smiled. "Let me help." He sent Shaun to practice dribbling around the pylons with the other kids.

Ian put the ball in front of Claire.
He watched as she kicked hard, and
the ball spun sideways
off the end of her shoe.
"See? That's not
where it should go,"
she said.

Ian bent down, took Claire's foot in his hand, and turned it a little. "Try using the side of your foot a bit more." He stood and smiled at her. "That face is too pretty to wear a frown. Let's see a smile."

Claire didn't mind being called pretty, but being pretty had nothing to do with playing soccer. She was getting a weird feeling. She didn't smile. Ian patted her back as she walked toward the other kids.

A few minutes later the whistle blew, and practice ended. "Good workout, team," Ian said. "See you next week."

The kids hurried off with their parents.

Claire's mom was on the other side of the field, talking to someone. Claire gathered up her sweater and water bottle and sat on the grass to wait. Then Ian came and sat right beside her.

"If you come early next week, I'll give you more one-to-one time. And Claire! Don't take soccer so seriously. It's supposed to be fun!" He tickled her in the ribs. Claire squirmed and moved sideways a bit.

"Sorry," he said. "But it's really your fault. You look so sad you make me want to tickle you," said Ian, leaning her way. "If you promise to keep it a secret, I'll tell you something."

"Why should it be a secret?" asked Claire.

"Because the other kids – probably their parents, too – might not like it if they find out you are my star player."

There it was again, the weird feeling. Only this time it was an *uh-oh* feeling.

Claire's mom arrived. "I'm sorry I kept you waiting, sweetheart," she said. "Let's go. Have you got everything?"

As they left, Ian called to Claire, "Don't forget what I told you. Come early next time, and we'll get those kicks working better."

"It's nice of Coach Ian to offer you extra help," Claire's mom said.

"I guess," said Claire, but keeping a secret about Ian's tickling didn't feel right. *And why am I Ian's star player?* she wondered. *I can't even kick the ball in a straight line!* Claire had some thinking to do. She sat on her front steps and worried until her mom called her in for dinner.

By recess the next morning, she was still confused. She decided to talk with Shaun and Nadia.

"Does Coach Ian make you guys feel kind of strange?"

"Strange how?" asked Shaun.

"Well he tells me I'm pretty, and he's always touching me. Yesterday he told me to keep it a secret."

Nadia frowned. "My dad says adults shouldn't ask kids to keep secrets about touch."

"What happened?" Shaun asked.

Claire wasn't sure she should tell, but she took a deep breath and hoped her friends would understand. "Ian touches and tickles me. He says I'm special – his favorite player, but that I shouldn't tell because people won't like it if they find out. But then he said I needed extra 'one-to-one help.' If am such a star, why do I need extra help?"

"Uh-oh," Shaun and Nadia said together.

"You better tell your mom," Nadia said.

"She thinks Ian's nice for giving me extra coaching. What if he really is just being nice?"

"What about the secret?" asked Shaun.

"Yeah! What about that?" Nadia added.

Claire didn't have an answer. But Nadia said secrets about touching weren't good.

That night, Claire went to her big sister's room and told her about everything: the touching and the secret, Ian working alone with her, and how she was his favorite player. "What do you think, Anna?"

"Sounds weird to me," said Anna, taking Claire's hand. "Let's talk to Mom."

"Will Ian be in trouble because of me? And what if the kids hate me because I'm his favorite?"

"If Ian gets into trouble it will be because of him, not you. And nobody's going to hate you. I promise."

After telling her story for the third time, Claire was upset. She wondered if she was somehow to blame. "What should I do, Mom?" Claire wanted to know.

"You have already done it!" said her mom, giving Claire a great big hug. "You listened to your feelings and realized they are important. I'm glad you told me this, and I believe you."

"Will Ian be angry with me?"

"Sweetheart, don't worry about Ian. No one should ever ask children to keep secrets about touching. Ian knows that. I'm so proud of you *and* your sister for coming to me."

Claire slept well that night.

The next morning was Saturday. Claire asked Shaun and Nadia over to play soccer in her backyard.

After a while they stopped for a break.

"Hey, Claire, what happened about the secret?" asked Nadia. "Did you talk to your mom?"

"Yep," said Claire. "You were right. She was glad I told her. And you'll never guess who will be coaching us next week."

"Who?" asked Shaun.

Claire's mom appeared with a tray of lemonade. "Me!" she laughed. "But I haven't played soccer in a long time."

"You'll be great, Mom," said Claire. "We'll give you a little practice – right now."

For Grown-ups

About Touch

Positive touch is an integral part of all relationships. Most importantly, children need to be sent a clear message that all touching can be talked about. Children who know they have the right to say "No" or to question how they've been touched gain valuable child abuse prevention skills. They need help identifying the differences between touch that feels good, touch that does not feel good, and touch that makes them feel uncomfortable. Touch may be a confusing issue for children because adults can give mixed messages; for example, parents might tell children to kiss someone goodnight when they don't want to, or when a child is spanked as punishment for hitting a sibling.

Parents can support their children in learning to talk about touching:

- **Talk about touch**: Openly discuss with children different kinds of touch and the feelings connected to touching.

- **Show respect**: Talk to children about liking and respecting their bodies, appreciating that they have the right to decide how they want to be touched.

- **Set an example**: Children need to know that all feelings are okay, and that problems can be solved without being physical and hurting one another.

- **There are no secrets**: Explain to children that no one should tell them to keep any kind of touch a secret – remember, all touching can be talked about.

- **Listen to your body**: Teach your children about the "uh-oh" feeling and help them identify adults they trust that they can talk to when they have a problem or a worry.

- **Show your love**: Hug your children – all children benefit from positive, nurturing touch.